The Wooden Horse

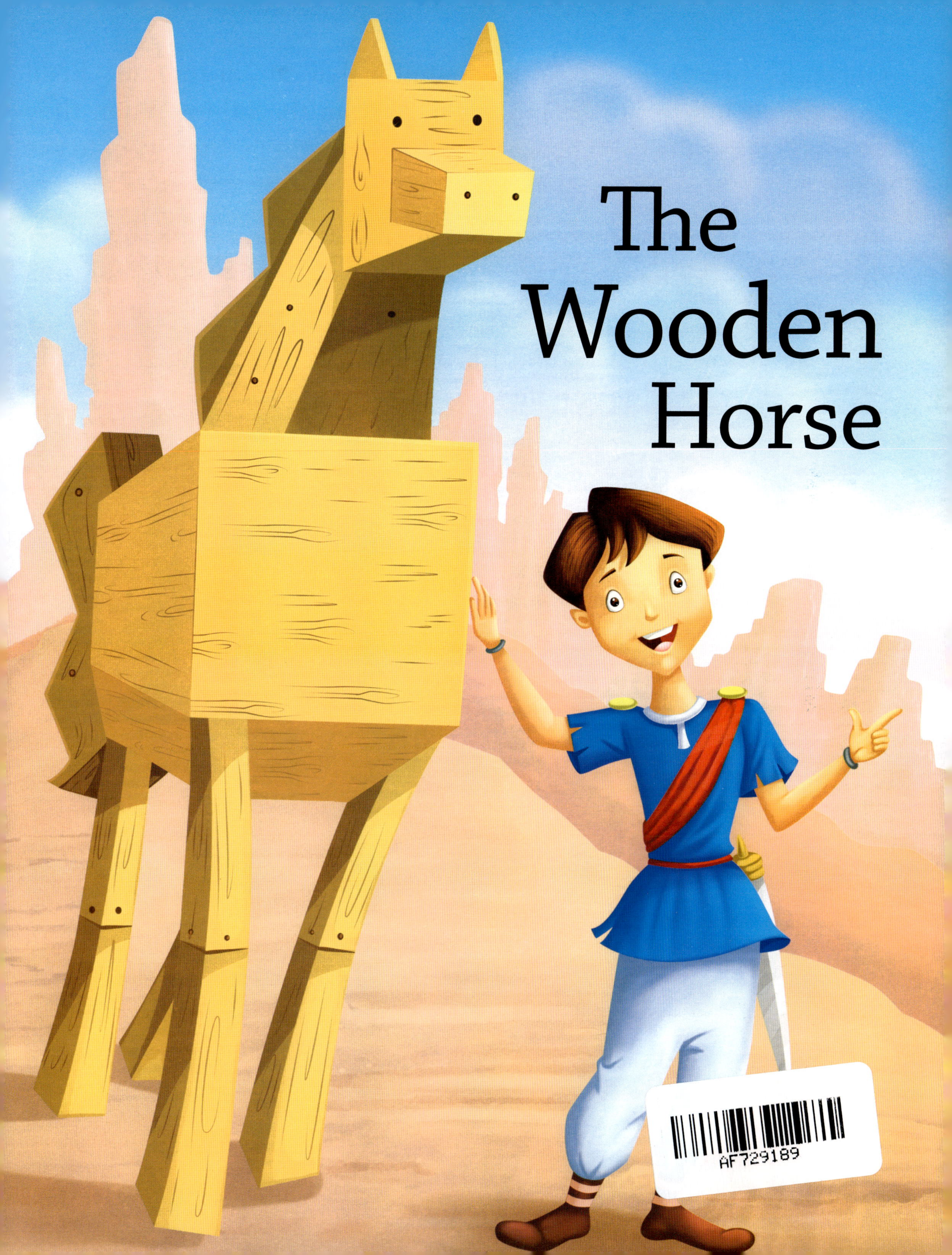

Once, a carpenter and a blacksmith had an argument. Each considered himself to be more skilful than the other. When they were unable to decide who was better among them, they went to the king.

'How can I pass judgment without seeing anything made by either of you?' said the king. 'Return in ten days with your work and then I shall judge.'

Ten days later, the blacksmith brought with him a huge iron fish. 'What can this do?' asked the king.

'It can float in the sea loaded with a hundred thousand sacks of grain,' said the blacksmith.

'Impossible! It will sink!' said the king. 'But anyway, load it with the said sacks of grain.' Once filled, the iron fish was launched. Surprisingly, the fish moved through the water with speed and efficiency.

Impressed, the king made the blacksmith a beadle of one of his districts. The carpenter then brought forth a wooden horse. Seeing it, the king said, 'Surely this is a child's toy?'

'Your Majesty, it's better than the iron fish,' said the carpenter. 'It has twenty-six screws on it. On loosening the first screw, the wooden horse will fly into the sky; on loosening the second screw, it will accelerate. On gradually loosening all the screws, it shall fly quickly than any bird.'

Hearing this, the young prince became curious. How he wished to fly the horse and see the world. He asked the king, 'Allow me to ride the horse.' But the king said sternly, 'No. Can it really fly? What if it falls to the ground?'

But the prince continued to pester the king, until he agreed. 'Alright, you can only try,' said the king. 'Fly slowly and only loosen the first screw.'

Agreeing to this, the little prince mounted the horse. He loosened the first screw, and at once the wooden horse rose into the air. He looked down and saw everything beneath him moving further away. Delighted, he began loosening one screw after another.

The wooden horse flew faster and faster and soon the prince was out of sight. After a while, on seeing another city beneath him, the prince gradually tightened the screws and the wooden horse slowed down before landing. What fun! To arrive in the twinkling of an eye in a new town!

While walked through the town, the prince saw people looking skyward in a square. Curious, he inquired. A man told him, 'To keep the princess safe, our king has had a mansion built by an immortal in the sky where the princess lives. Every day, the king goes to meet her. We are waiting for his return.'

Hearing this, the prince had made up his mind to see this palace. Next day, he mounted his horse and reached the palace in the sky. It was matchless!

No sooner had the prince entered the palace that he saw the princess. She too was surprised to see him. As they talked, they fell in love. The prince learnt that the princess was tired of staying alone. 'I shall come to take you tomorrow,' said the prince. The princess agreed. Next day, as promised the prince came to take away the princess.

They had been flying for a while, when the princess cried, 'I forgot to bring the two precious stones my mother had given me. Let me return.'

'We are already a long way from the palace,' said the prince but he landed the horse. He added, 'I'll wait for you here. Go to the palace on the wooden horse and return soon.' The princess then mounted the horse and flew away.

Meanwhile, the king had come to meet his daughter. When he did not see her, he was at his wit's end. It was at this moment that the princess returned to the palace on the wooden horse.

Seeing her, the king made her confess everything. Angry, he locked her in his palace and kept the horse in his store room. Meanwhile, the prince kept waiting for the princess. At last, he decided to go towards the princess' palace.

On the other hand, the king had decided to marry his daughter. He sent an invitation to a far off prince to come and take his bride. Meanwhile, the prince was lost in a vast desert. The boundless stretch of desert with towering sand dunes, unbearable heat and no food had left the prince fatigued. Tired, hungry and thirsty, he dragged himself to the top of a large dune.

Suddenly, the prince slipped and rolled down the sand dune. When he stopped, he was in an orchard filled with fruit trees. He ate a few peaches, hungrily and fell asleep.

When the prince woke up, he saw that he had a long white beard. He was troubled. But suddenly he felt terribly hungry and quickly plucked some pears. Again he fell asleep. When he woke up, he felt horns on his head! 'How terrible I look!' he said. 'The princess will never recognize me like this!' Saying so, he started crying. Soon, exhausted, he fell sleep.

While he slept, the prince dreamt of an old man who said, 'Son, eat the fallen, dried peaches and pears and your beard and horns will disappear.'

Startled, the prince woke up. At once, he picked a few dried pears and peaches and ate them. Sure enough, when he finished eating them, his beard and horns had vanished. He was happy. Then, thinking something he wove a basket of twigs and filled it half with dry peaches and pears and half with fresh ones. He then rushed out of the orchard.

The prince was again in the desert. Again, he walked through the desert for seven days and nights, eating only the dried pears and peaches. His dress, by now, was torn and filled with sand. He did not look like a prince!

Finally the prince reached a highway. He walked for hours towards the princess' city when suddenly he heard a man shouting orders far behind him. It was a retinue behind him. As they passed him by, he saw soldiers and courtiers riding on magnificent horses in full armour.

The soldiers surrounded a wooden carriage with glass windows on all four sides and driven by white horses. Suddenly, the carriage stopped and a soldier asked him, 'Would you sell your fruits to our prince? He is hungry.'

'But these fruits are my food,' said the prince.

Hearing this, the prince inside the carriage shouted, 'Pay whatever he asks!' Saying this, he held a bag of gold coins out of the carriage window.

Then, as the prince held out pears and peaches for the prince, he learnt that the prince in the carriage was going to marry the princess in the town ahead. The prince was stunned. The bride was the princess he loved! Soon the retinue moved ahead.

After some miles, the retinue stopped when their prince started crying loudly. Courtiers and soldiers rushed to his carriage. They saw no prince but a monster with a beard and two horns in the carriage. Panic-stricken, they waited for the fruit-seller to pass. When the fruit-seller caught up with them, they asked, 'What kind of fruit did you sell our prince? He has turned into a monster!'

Seeing the monster inside the carriage, the prince was delighted. But he calmly said, 'I eat the same fruit each day. Nothing has happened to me!' The soldiers and courtiers could say nothing to this. They were worried for the princess would not marry their prince looking like this.

Finally, a courtier said, 'We must find a handsome young man and disguise him as the prince. If we manage to take the princess to our kingdom, she would be at our mercy.' Everyone agreed to this plan. In the end, they persuaded the fruit-seller to pose as their prince. The fruit-seller agreed.

Minutes later, the prince was inside the carriage posing as the other, while the prince with horns and beard had his face veiled and he rode on a horse. Further, he was instructed to keep its face hidden. When they reached the city, the king welcomed them grandly. Immediately, preparations for the marriage started.

Initially, the princess was not ready to marry but when she saw the prince, she was delighted. It was because the groom was the prince she loved. The prince also told her how he had managed to come here. And then they planned to escape. The prince's idea was that after the wedding, she should ask her father for the wooden horse before she left with him. The princess agreed.

After the wedding when the prince and princess were about to depart, the princess requested her father to give her the wooden horse. Reluctantly, the king agreed.

The princess and the prince journeyed with the retinue for several days, unable to escape. Days later, they were approaching the other prince' city. 'We must leave now,' said the princess. Meanwhile, the townspeople were coming out of the city to welcome the prince and his bride. Seeing the courtiers and the soldiers distracted, the prince grabbed the wooden horse and asked the princess to sit behind him. Immediately, he loosened one screw on the horse' neck and they whooshed towards the sky before they could be stopped.

Soon, they reached safely in the prince's palace. The king, the prince's father, had meanwhile blamed his son's disappearance on the carpenter and was about to put the unfortunate man to death. But before that could be done the king saw his son. He was overjoyed.

Understanding the whole situation, the prince said, 'Father, the carpenter's wooden horse is amazing. Without it, I wouldn't have seen other countries and found such a beautiful bride. He should be awarded handsomely.'

Immediately, the carpenter was released. The king apologized to him and gave the carpenter a large sum of money to perfect his craft. The wooden horse remained with the prince who often travelled on it.

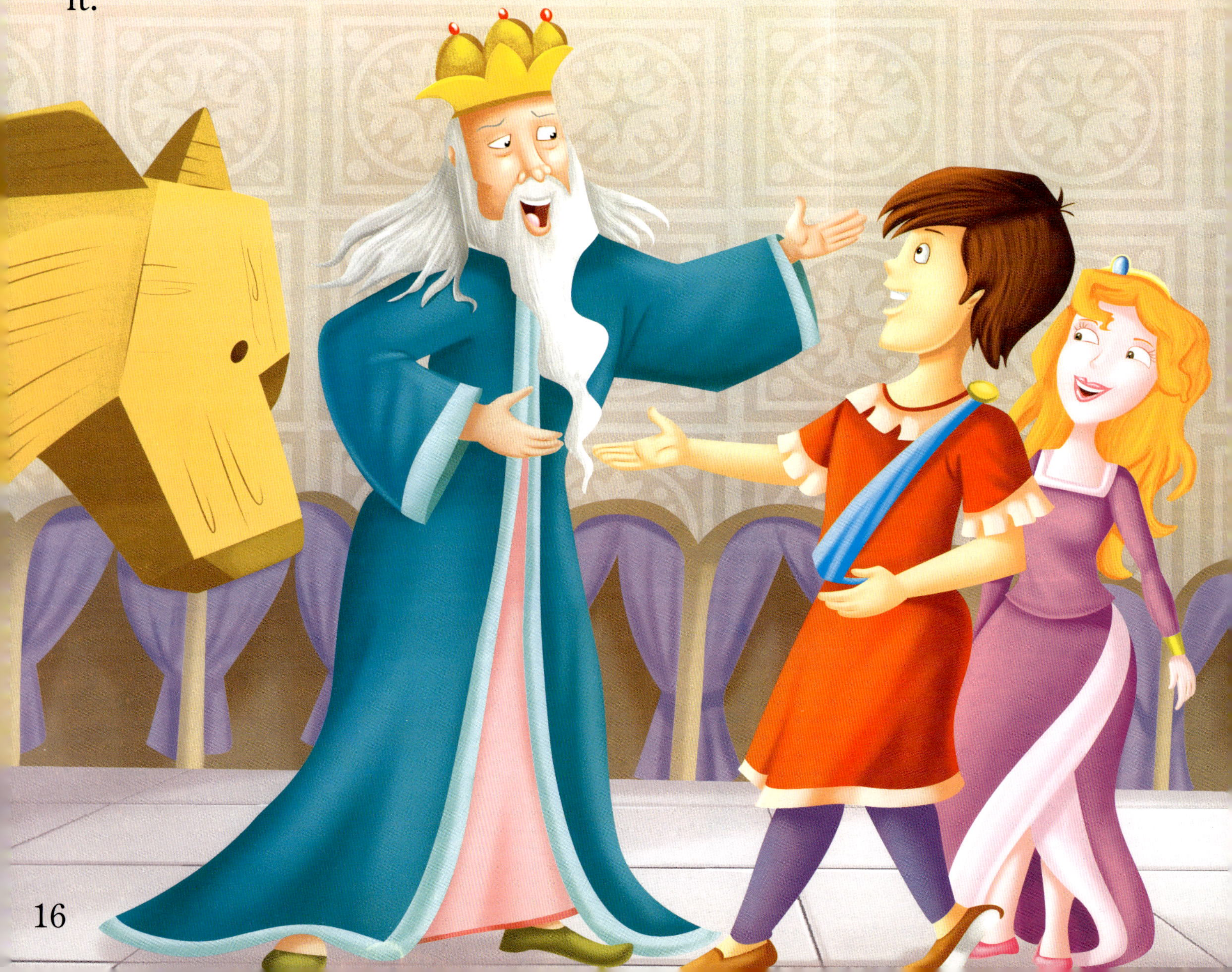